A CHILD'S GUIDE TO CALMING DOWN

Written by **Dr. Amanda DeSua**
Illustrated by John Konecny

This book belongs to:

_____

Published by Orange Hat Publishing 2016
ISBN 978-1-943331-16-1

Copyrighted © 2016 by **Dr. Amanda DeSua**
All Rights Reserved
Frog Slime
Written by Dr. Amanda DeSua
Illustrated by John Konecny

This publication and all contents within may not be reproduced or transmitted in any part or in its entirety without the written permission of the author.

Printed in the United States of America

www.orangehatpublishing.com

To my wonderful daughters, Catalina and Dahlia, who have shown me the power of resilience, the beauty of self-control, and that mistakes are really opportunities to learn and grow.

There once lived a little girl named Daisy.

Daisy probably had a lot in common with boys and girls just like you. She loved ice cream, she always had fun when she went swimming, she thought little baby animals were super cute, and sometimes she got really, really <u>frustrated</u>.

Her cat, Zuzu, who scratched her too much made her frustrated.

Her older brother who wouldn't let her in his room made her frustrated.

Her mom asking her to clean her room before she could go out and play made her frustrated.

Even her teacher, Mr. Sunshine, made her frustrated, especially when it was close to lunch and Daisy was super duper hungry.

In fact, Daisy felt frustrated so often she even named her frustration - **FROG SLIME**.

FROG SLIME would appear when Daisy didn't expect it. Sometimes she would be eating dinner and her dad would start talking about football and then she would remember how at school she was picked last to play in the football game, and then when she scored a touchdown for the opposite team everyone yelled at her. First she got sad and then FROG SLIME arrived.

FROG SLIME seemed to coat poor Daisy's mind in sticky, green slime. The parts of her brain that used to help her stay calm were covered in gooey gunk! Instead of calming down, she slammed her fork down and ran up to her room.

Life went on like this for a while. When FROG SLIME arrived Daisy felt her body tighten up, her face got hot, her tummy hurt a little, and she felt like she would explode!

In fact, one day when Daisy was in the hallway at school some of her classmates were singing a really annoying song really, really loud. Her head hurt and she asked them to stop. They sang louder and ignored Daisy even though she had asked nicely.

Her body tightened, her face got hot, her tummy hurt, and **FROG SLIME** struck again! "Stop singing that stupid song you jerks!" Daisy yelled.

That night, a very exhausted Daisy lay her head down on her purple, fluffy pillow and had the most amazing dream. She traveled through a long rainbow tunnel until she arrived at a beautiful waterfall. The waterfall sparkled in the sun and had the most clear, crisp water. The type of water that could clean even something as sticky and gooey as FROG SLIME.

Daisy began to wander around, smelling the flowers and listening to the birds chirping over the sound of rushing water. Then she heard the birds' chirping turn into a peaceful tune. The song echoed in Daisy's mind as she slept through the night.

When you are frustrated, stop and wait.
Just remember deep breaths are great.
Try to count from 1 to 10.
You may even need to do it again.
Exercise, draw a picture, or take a break.
You can make a good choice for goodness sake!
Stay safe with coping skills each and every day.
Calm, brave, and safe your body will stay.

The next morning as Daisy brushed her teeth, her brand new princess toothbrush fell right in the toilet! Daisy felt her face get warm, but before **FROG SLIME** covered her brain in gooey slime she thought of her dream. She was reminded of the song the birds chirped.

When you are frustrated, stop and wait.
Just remember deep breaths are great.
Try to count from 1 to 10.
You may even need to do it again.
Exercise, draw a picture, or take a break.
You can make a good choice for goodness sake!
Stay safe with coping skills each and every day.
Calm, brave, and safe your body will stay.

Daisy took a deep breath and told herself, "It is only a toothbrush. This is a small problem that is easy to fix." And then she wandered into the kitchen to ask her mom for another toothbrush.

Later that day at school, Daisy realized she forgot her homework on the bus. When she told Mr. Sunshine he suggested she work on the homework during free play time. Daisy's tummy started to hurt. She loved free play time. Just as she was about to roll her eyes at Mr. Sunshine, she remembered...

When you are frustrated, stop and wait.
Just remember deep breaths are great.
Try to count from 1 to 10.
You may even need to do it again.
Exercise, draw a picture, or take a break.
You can make a good choice for goodness sake!
Stay safe with coping skills each and every day.
Calm, brave, and safe your body will stay.

Daisy stopped, and counted 1, 2, 3, 4, 5, 6, 7, 8, 9, 10 and thought "I'll get free play again tomorrow. I'll be ok."

It seemed like FROG SLIME visited Daisy less often. She felt more in control of her body and knew that the birds in her dream had taught her a lesson that would help her throughout the rest of her life.

She knew to stop and calm down before making a decision and that sometimes little problems feel like big problems. Daisy still got frustrated, but she knew she could work through it and de-slime her mind!

Discussion Questions

1. What happens to your body when you become angry or frustrated?

2. What are some coping skills you like to use?

3. Daisy had to decide if her toothbrush falling in the toilet was a big problem or little problem. How can you tell the difference between a big problem and a little problem?

4. When Daisy was upset about missing play time, she thought in her mind "I'll get free play again tomorrow. I'll be ok." What does your self-talk sound like? What can you say in your mind that could help you calm down?

5. Daisy named her frustration Frog Slime. If you named your frustration, what name would you choose?

CPSIA information can be obtained
at www.ICGtesting.com
Printed in the USA
BVHW02n0038080818
523870BV00005B/50/P